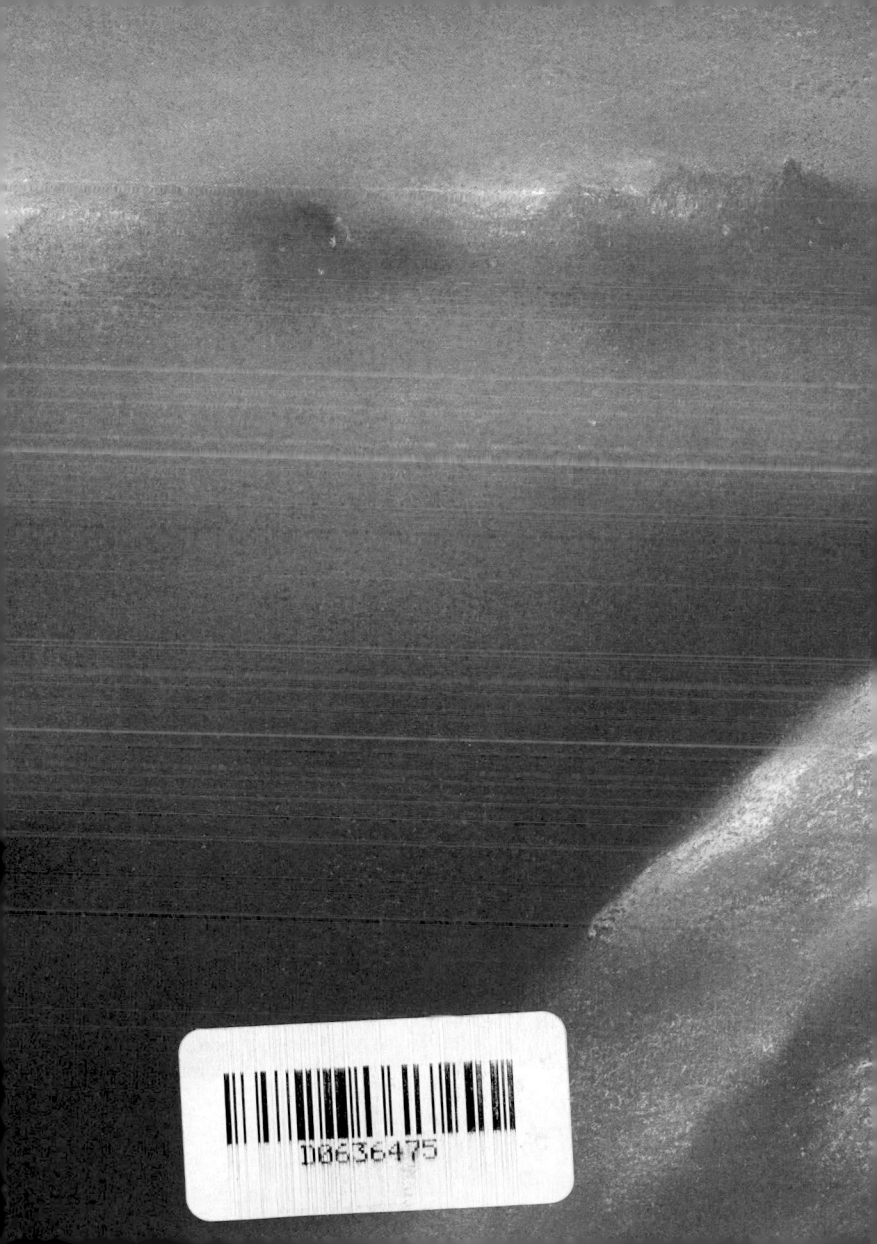

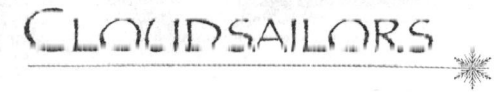

CLOUDSAILORS

Also by Hugh Montgomery

The Voyage of the Arctic Tern

CLOUDSAILORS

Hugh Montgomery

illustrated by Liz Pyle

WALKER BOOKS
AND SUBSIDIARIES
LONDON · BOSTON · SYDNEY · AUCKLAND

First published 2005 by Walker Books Ltd

87 Vauxhall Walk, London SE11 5HJ

2 4 6 8 10 9 7 5 3 1

Text © 2005 Hugh Montgomery

Illustrations © 2005 Liz Pyle

The right of Hugh Montgomery and Liz Pyle to be identified as author and illustrator respectively of this work has been asserted by them in accordance with the Copyright, Designs and Patents Act 1988

This book has been typeset in Truesdell and Papyrus

Printed in China

British Library Cataloguing in Publication Data: a catalogue record for this book is available from the British Library

ISBN 1-84428-645-2

www.walkerbooks.co.uk

"There is nothing too small
for a truly big man."

This book is dedicated to James Nelson,

and to his grandson, Oscar Nelson.

May the boy be even a tenth of the man.

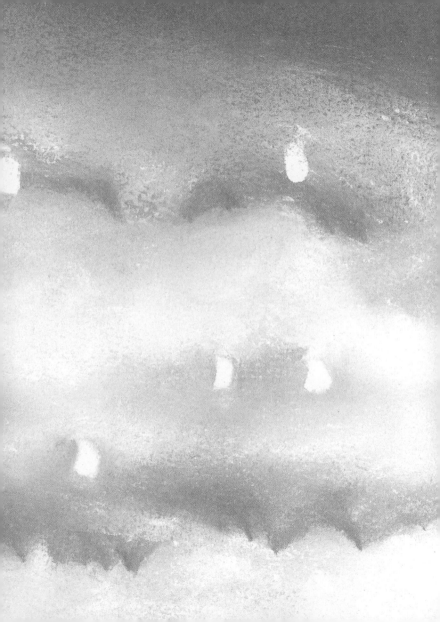

Contents

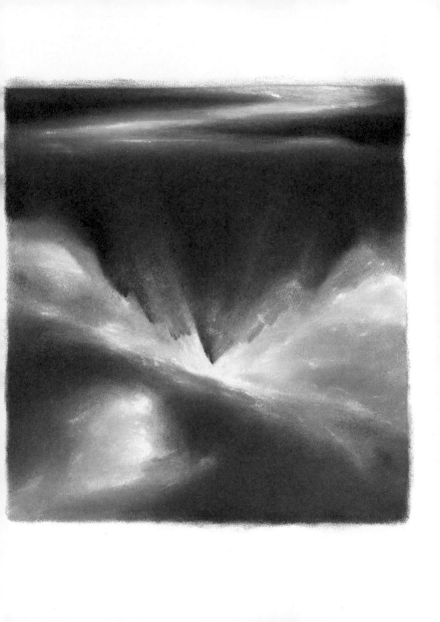

The Myth of the Mountainfolk

IN THE BEGINNING, *far far in the distant past, before the moon existed or time itself had come to be, the skies were of fire and black, and burned like oil on a midnight sea. But in the cold void of space, the flames were tamed and sapped of strength. And as they cooled, the Earth was born.*

She was young and beautiful and warm, clad in pure air, and bathed in gold by the summer sun. Her mountains rose in massive black majesty, and in winter the snows that fell upon her were as white as light itself. In spring, meltwater distilled from the icicles, spilled from the peaks, and tumbled clear and clean through the rivers, tinkling like crystal against the boulders, bringing life to the plains and valleys below.

Amidst this beauty dwelled the Menfolk. Some settled high in the mountains in hidden caves hewn from the cliffs, clad in pelt of fox and wolf for warmth. Others lived in the lowland valleys, where they tended the fertile soil. But they were one people, and would travel from high to low, low to high, sharing the wealth of root and berry, never taking more from the Earth than she could afford to give.

Time passed and, slowly, the Mountainfolk and the Lowlanders each grew into the place of their dwelling, as the ivy grows inseparable from the branches of the ageing oak. The Lowlanders travelled less to the mountains, where the air was sparse and thin. And the less they climbed, the less they thought of the mountains until, one day, they were no longer able to ascend at all. Many moved from the valleys, to settle the distant coastal plains. And with time, they came to forget the mountains and those who dwelled among them.

Meanwhile, the Mountainfolk above grew accustomed to the harshness of the heights, relishing the delicacy of the air, cold and fragile, and finding the heavy vapours of the lowlands ever harder to breathe. In time, they could spend no more than hours in the valley floor before, coughing and weakened, they were forced to retreat. Yet food was scarce so high in the mountains, and they continued to forage among the fields and stores of the Lowlanders below. They moved at night, when the mountain slopes were frozen and safe from sudden avalanche, and when moonshadows would shield them from sight. For they were a shy and gentle people, grown fearful of the ways of the Lowlanders, and anxious what discovery might bring.

And as these Mountainfolk foraged below, the night air cooled, and a thick cloud rose and lapped the shores of the mountain slopes. Under the yellow light of the rising moon, those who remained above took yeti claw and tooth and fashioned glittering coracles of ice. These they launched from ramps of snow to sail upon the sea of cloud, ferrying the returning bounty from peak to peak. But such work had to be done before dawn, before the heat of the rising sun could strike. For then the cloud became turbulent, boiling violently and spilling the unwary from their craft.

But things were changing in the Lowlanders' world. Those who had settled on the coastal plains had swelled in number, and with them their appetite for food and fuel. Their cities grew, consuming everything around them. Trees were felled, whole forests cleared. Fires burned day and night. Fumes and phosphor filled the air, thickening to a distant smear of yellow paste above the towns. And the Mountainfolk shook their heads in disbelief.

Before long the valley air became acrid, foul to the taste and cruel to the lungs of the Mountainfolk. Their descents became ever more brief, and their dwellings were abandoned as they retreated ever higher. Soon, only the strongest could descend to forage. Food became scarce. In desperation, they took to harvesting summer lichen from the rocks, drying and storing it for the winter. But this was not enough and, with time, the weak succumbed. Faced with starvation, they sought refuge in distant mountain ranges, fleeing in a fleet of glittering ice-coracles, praying that they might make landfall before sunrise.

✳

Such is the myth of the
Mountainfolk as it was told
to Sundeep by his
grandfather, Helygen.

And it is said that in each
myth lies a truth, like a grain
of sand within a pearl.

Suspended Animation

DESPITE THE CHILL AIR, the bee took the straight line up the valley, beating its wings furiously for warmth. Ahead, the black mountain stood sentry. Beneath, the world, snap-frozen. Above, the night sky watching, as black as a raven's eye.

On and up. Through the lowlands, where wreathes of vapour coiled. Over crystallized stems and frosted granite boulders, which sparkled in the moonlight.

On and up, as a wash of white light bleached the eastern horizon. Up, until the eggshell sky cracked along the razor edge of the crags and a trickle of white leaked into the valley.

On and up, as the orange furnace-spill of dawn flushed life from every stone and shelter, the chorus of awakening drowning out the roar of the sunlight.

And on this tumult, the bee was borne aloft, fat as apricot, light as mallow, golden as toffee, lacing its own lazy tracery of honey-scent over the baking soil.

The climb complete, it levelled over the fertile plains before swooping into the meadow, where flowers dripped sweet nectar and fat pollen butter-balls. And here, it gorged upon the waves of petals, until giddy and sated in the strong afternoon sun.

And then to the house of the orphan boy, to meander amongst paprika-roasted rocks and rest on the trellis draped in pink-peach, orange and vine.

To wander the garden, where its continuous drunken mumble caused the orphan boy Sundeep to pause.

Pause as Meirwen, his mother, once had as she tended the vine. Pause as his father, Morwen, once had, smiling and welcoming the visiting bee with a comical flourish of the hand. Pause as old Helygen once had; the grandfather who had aged amongst the ancient olive trees, bark and bone together, twisting and wracked, creaking and cracked, bent for shade against the noon sun. The grandfather who had rested his weary hand upon Sundeep's head, and finally his weary soul amongst the blackened fruit which covered the soft soil.

And, as Sundeep paused, his tears were spilled. For now he had no one.

The bee had turned for home long before darkness fell; was far down the valley as the sun settled over the skyline and tendril shadows reached silently for the valley floor.

The orphan boy stood shivering and alone, his hand shading his eyes against the final glow of the sun. He turned to walk slowly to the old stone house. To close the door behind him. To plead the embers of fire to life.

And, high, high above, among the cold black crags, past the glacier tongue and the razor teeth of the lower ridges, unseen in the maw of the Mountain, an old man with a wiry white beard paused a while longer. Saw the boy safely into his house. Watched as the first trace of smoke rose from the chimney. Sighed, then lowered his head as sparks of hot ash floated upwards.

And at the valley end, the bee drifted alone, an orange mote afloat upon unseen seas.

※

The Lost Family

❄

OUTSIDE, the temperature was well below zero. Across the glacial plain, the river swarmed with ice needles, their agitation preventing it from freezing solid. Even so, a fragile lace of ice would cover the edging boulders come morning.

Inside, Sundeep lay still, his gritty eyes screwed tightly shut, for if he concentrated hard, he was no longer alone.

He thought of his parents, and smiled as they chased him again through the meadows, racing the bee in its flight, laughing with the sun. He watched as they set off with packs and axes to climb the Mountain. Went with them to the

Secret Place, sitting with his father while his mother climbed on.

He thought of his mother, Meirwen, her eyes like tigerstones, golden and flecked with rust. He felt the firmness of her grasp as she lifted him, swung him, held him and laughed with him, her hair suffused with the evening light. He remembered her standing alone to savour the dawn, eyes shut, half-smiling, as she rolled the chill air upon her tongue. He remembered, too, that one special, dreadful morning. How she had stood for hour upon hour, looking anxiously over the distant mountain. His own excitement as a sudden shower of shooting stars had streaked across the sky and fallen to Earth. And how she had cried, immune to the comfort of husband or son.

And then she was gone, walking from their home into a winter's storm, never to return. Leaving him alone with his father.

He thought of his father, Morwen. They had grown closer together, the day Meirwen died. Grown older together too, for in that year his father stooped ever more beneath his load, and Sundeep came to shoulder a greater share. And as time passed, Morwen ceased to climb the Mountain, his heavy heart weighing him to the valley floor.

But then, one day, his eyes drifted again to the peaks. He toyed with his crampons, eyeing the valley edge for signs of storm. He prepared his pack and axes, and then was gone, bearing a rucksack of food, and returning unladen before dawn.

He made a second trip and a third. And more. Until that final morning when he had risen earlier than ever before. Long before the heat of the sun could hammer the snowfields on the high mountain, releasing frozen stones to spin free and strike him. Before the melting slopes could pour down thundering avalanche to bury the trespasser below.

Sundeep had heard his father rise.

Heard the coarse wool hush as he sank his socks into his old boots.

Heard the creak of the leather as the laces were pulled tight.

Felt the lightness of lips upon his forehead as he pretended to sleep, and heard his father's last, whispered words. "I must do what is right for those I have failed. May you, and they, forgive me."

And listened as his father's hoarse breath and steady steps receded.

He remembered how he got up and stood through the cold darkness of the early morning, staring at the high mountain as his mother had before him. And how, that time, only a single shooting star marked the dawn. And he, too, wept as his mother had, knowing that his father would not return.

And now, as Sundeep slipped towards slumber, soft cloud surrounded him and shooting stars sparkled past, carrying the memory of his family away.

Grandfather's Story

S UNDEEP STIRRED, and woke from his sleep. The night was treacle-black and bitter as bark. Endless and lonely, now that even his grandfather had gone. His father's father. Helygen.

For Helygen, the death of his own flesh and blood had been more than he could bear, for no man should outlive his son. But together he and Sundeep had struggled on; pruned the vines, picked the lush fruit, pressed the olives. But in their work there was no joy, for life held no beauty any more.

And then the old man, too, was dead.

Sundeep began to weep, as still-warm memories washed about him. Submerged him.

He remembered sitting beside the old man at nightfall, as the dying sun bled golden resin from the ridges, embedding all in stiffening cold, like ants in amber. The windows of the cottage were already glazed with frost. Inside, the fire snapped greedily and spat red embers across the hearth. Beside it, his face flickering in the light of the flames, Sundeep crouched and stirred the pot, as old Helygen hung up his worn woollen coat and wheezed warming mists into his cupped hands.

Side by side they ate in silence, plunging buttered crusts into their rough wooden bowls. Afterwards, they sat together in silence too, as the logs settled bright and watchful in the grate.

And as so often, Sundeep's eyes were drawn to the mantelpiece. To the small glass perfume bottle, draped with a silver chain and locket. And to the strange objects that lay beside it. What they were, he had never been told. The scimitar was the length of a foot, its edge as sharp as split flint. Beside it, the white pick was as thick as a thumb, curved and tapered to a needlepoint.

And above them hung the smudged charcoal lines of the picture, framed in peeling bark. It showed mountain mists and rocky peaks and coracles carved of ice afloat upon seas of cloud as people busied themselves with their moorings. The mythical Mountainfolk. As a child, he had been told their tale. How they had retreated to the heights as the Lowlanders grew in number. How they still lived there in secret, coming down at night to forage.amongst these very farms.

And when very young and foolish, he had believed these tales to be true.

※

Helygen looked down at his grandson and gathered the orphan boy more tightly to him, and the heavy blanket more closely about them. Sundeep pressed his cheek firmly to his grandfather's chest, comforted by the bristles of the old man's beard, the animal warmth of his breath.

Outside, a harsh wind slapped the door and rattled the catches, brief flurries of snow striking the windows like handfuls of flailed rice. They held their silence, Sundeep staring into the fire. Then, hoarse and quiet, he whispered to his grandfather, "Tell me again of my parents."

Helygen smiled and ruffled the boy's hair. Each night it was the same. And yet talking of Morwen and Meirwen somehow brought them back to life. For them both. And so he began.

"Your mother was an only child, and so beautiful that all about her felt touched with joy and light and mountain air. Morwen, my son, was on the upper trails of the Mountain when first they met. He came back that day so full of happiness that I knew at once they should marry. And so they did – he the silent thick-set Lowlander, and she the laughing elfin dancer. And after their marriage, they continued to climb together high on the Mountain, with heavy packs and light hearts. But nothing brought them as much joy as your arrival, young Sundeep. For you bore your father's frame, yet the music of your soul was your mother's. And, when you were old enough, you went with them onto the Mountain. Climbed with them to the Secret Place."

Sundeep thought in silence, remembering those trips. How he stumbled beside them up the track, singing the Song of the Valley as they went. How he was carried to the

Keyhole, crawling deep within to enter the Secret Place. Once inside, he and his father would read the rocks by candlelight while Meirwen climbed on alone. Then, as the day drew to a close, she would return, her pack empty, and they would go down the Mountain, Sundeep swaddled in sleep and contentment. He remembered half-waking to ask where she had been. They would answer with raised eyebrows and distant smiles, and the promise that one day, when he was older, they would tell him.

But "one day" never came. Now his parents were dead, and still he did not know. There was so much that he did not know. Tears welled in his eyes, and he looked up at old Helygen.

"Grandfather? Where did my mother go from the Secret Place? And if they loved me, why did they leave me? Surely they cannot be dead?"

His grandfather looked down at the boy. He said softly, "They are dead."

"But why did they abandon me?"

Helygen rocked Sundeep against him. "They did not abandon you, but lost their lives for others. One day, you will understand." He held the boy close. "And you are not abandoned. You have me, and I will never leave you."

"But when will I know what happened to them, Grandfather?"

The old man paused, then answered gently, "When you are older. For with knowledge of the truth may come decisions. Decisions which cannot be made when young."

Sundeep's eyes were drifting shut once more. "Tell me, Grandfather…"

Helygen lifted his grandson, then paused, his tone serious and his gaze intense. "Each picture tells a story, young Sundeep. The answer lies in the mountains."

And here, Sundeep's grandfather ended as he always did, lightly touching the boy's head with his lips.

Helygen's voice had been receding for some time, yet Sundeep struggled to raise his head from half-sleep. "But what became of them?" His grandfather kissed him lightly once more. Sundeep was mumbling now. "Shall I ever learn the truth?"

Helygen whispered his reply. "That, young Sundeep, will depend upon you."

And as he was carried to his bed, Sundeep caught one last glimpse of the curious objects above the fire and of the picture that hung over them. And inside that picture, as he passed, an old man seemed to turn his head and smile.

※

The Quest

BUT NOW OLD HELYGEN WAS GONE, and Sundeep was lying here all alone. What was there left for him? Myths of Mountainfolk and coracles of ice, and the lingering memories of his own family: of their trips to the Secret Place; and of his mother's lone climbs onwards up the Mountain.

And beyond myths and memories? The perfume jar and locket, the strange objects upon the mantelpiece, and the faded charcoal picture above it. And even these he would soon have to leave, for he could never tend the orchard and the vines alone. Helygen had kept his promise that Sundeep would never be abandoned. Near the coast dwelled an ageing cousin and her family, who had long since vowed to care for him should his grandfather die. He had already received word from them that he was expected. In a week, he would leave for the coast, where the weather was warmer and life was more comfortable. Where he could forget, for ever, the harshness of the mountain way.

He knew that they were kindly folk, that he would want for nothing. And he knew that, in time, he would come to love them as his family, and to love the place he would soon make his home.

But before Sundeep left, he *had* to know where his mother had gone when she climbed on from the Secret Place. Had to know, too, why his father had left him. And how they had both died. He had only one week in which to make these discoveries.

He opened his eyes, smearing his tears with the back of a hand, the thoughts of his family still raw in his mind.

What was it Helygen had said?

"Each picture tells a story."

He furrowed his brow.

Each picture tells a story.

He walked to the only picture in the house, and stared at the faded faces of the mythical Mountainfolk, and at the crystal ice-craft in which they sailed.

What was the story in this picture?

He looked more closely, but could see no obvious clues. Was he missing something?

He hesitated before lifting the picture from its hook. Despite his care, the ageing bark frame sprang free, the picture within drifting to the floor in autumnal sweeps.

He picked it up.

It seemed to have been etched on beaten bark, or perhaps the skin of some animal. Its surface was of uneven ochre, and rough to the touch. The lines upon it were charcoal, yet held nothing new; no signature from the artist, no fine detail missed when viewed from afar.

He turned the picture over.

And there it was.

His breath snatched in his chest.

Another drawing.

✳

He knelt and examined it. Not so much one drawing, perhaps, as several, spreading stepwise across the page. In effect, a crude map. To the left, a cottage. *His* cottage, the orchard and vines outside clearly identifiable. Upwards and to the right, another image: the Secret Place seen from a narrow mouth of rock and recognizable at once. But beyond that, the places were unfamiliar.

Some sort of crack, choked with boulders.

A hanging ledge, crusted with snow.

A huge cliff of ice, with someone pressed against its face.

And then another view from the summit of a mountain. *The* Mountain: for there below, visible in the valley, was his house.

And beneath these images, words in an ancient and shaking hand:

> *Meirwen, with gratitude and love and gifts*
> *of tooth and claw – for Sundeep, your son.*

He looked again at the strange, curved objects upon the mantelpiece. The brown scimitar with its razor edge. The white cylinder with its needle-sharp point. A claw and a tooth? For *him*?

He thought again of old Helygen's words. "The answer lies in the mountains, young Sundeep…"

It was then that the urgency came upon him. His muscles tautened, his breath quickened. His mouth became dry.

For this *was* "one day". Now he *was* "older".

He would seek the answer in the mountains, would learn the mystery of his mother and father's deaths.

He would set out this very day, for in just a week he would leave for the coast. And would not return.

Sundeep put the picture back in its frame. Reaching into the wicker basket, he fed timber scraps to the starving fire, which leapt to life with a snap and a roar.

He moved with purpose now: coarse wool socks, first thin, then thick, then thicker still. Oiled-wool sweaters and oiled-wool hat; rough coat, thick gloves.

From above the fire, he took Meirwen's two wood-handled axes. From under his bed, her old tarpaulin pack, its aged leather straps stiff in their iron buckles.

From the pantry, fruit and olives and cheese and flask. Fuel and kindling.

And he walked from the house, not once looking back.

But watched all the while.

For high above, hunched on his eyrie ledge, an old man tugged his beard, and nodded.

"At last," he said. "He comes."

✳

The Secret Place

IT WAS ONLY MID-EVENING but already the valley was still. Sundeep moved through silence, scattering seeds of sound.

The scrape of his boot on char-black stone.

The huff of his breath, the crackle as it froze to a plume of frost around him.

The lathe-shave snick of cloth on cloth as he swung his arms.

At each hairpin of the path, he paused. Below, the black valley slowly appeared to lengthen, the central stream a mercury dribble. Above, the darkened face of the Mountain loomed closer. He stamped his feet. Flexed his fingers. The temperature was falling. He moved on.

An hour. Two. And now the first signs of the approaching snowline: occasional grey smears of ice beneath the boulders, patches of snowy crust scattered here and there, the last crystals of winter clustered in the hollows.

The path wound to the left. Sundeep cast an eye over his shoulder, before stooping and slipping to the right. Round the single thornbush, and up the short steep scramble to a narrow ledge on the cliff face. Edge to the right. And there it was. A narrow keyhole in the rock ahead, into which a small adult might squeeze. He pushed his pack ahead of him and crawled inside.

The slot was no more than twelve feet long and hewn so skilfully as to appear entirely natural. Its rough surface was slippery with ice, and Sundeep struggled as the canvas of his pack snagged on the walls. But he pressed on, down the gentle slope, and through the final choke of fallen rock at its exit. Standing, he brushed stone fragments from his damp knees and paused in wonder at the magic of the Secret Place.

He stood at the rim of a basin some two hundred feet across, hollowed from the core of the mountain, its floor strewn with giant boulders. Between them, a maze of small paths, inconsequences and echoes. Above, a chimney; a thousand feet of sheer black wall, roofed by sky. Oily yellow moonlight drizzled down, casting the boulders into pencilled relief. Around the walls, strange quartz hexagons split the light in a shifting kaleidoscope as he moved. And the only sound was the hiss of his breath

He had not been here for many years, for the climbs had ceased with the death of his mother. His grandfather had never been with them. Like most ordinary men, Helygen would have struggled at such height, for the air was too thin to breathe with ease. Trailing a hand over the familiar rocks to his left, Sundeep reached a particular boulder; a looming mass of granite with a scooped underside that formed a sloping roof high enough for a child to stand. Taller now, Sundeep stooped in order to move forwards. Ahead, on the ground, lay three small rounded stones, their upper surfaces polished smooth over the years. Sundeep put down his pack, and took his usual place, sitting as he had with his father when they read the rocks.

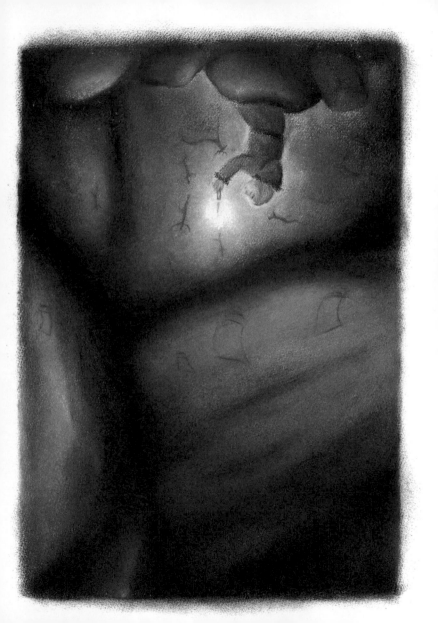

Perhaps his mother had paused here on the day she died.

Perhaps his father had done the same.

The kindling would not take easily, for the air was thin. The candle was a frozen white finger, and its wick fizzled and spluttered at first. When the flame had steadied, Sundeep fixed the light on a ledge in a spill of hot wax. From his flask, he poured thick sweet tea, clasping the cup in his gloved hands for comfort and warmth. And as the steam rose around him, and his face flickered yellow in the flame, he shivered. Not for the cold, but for the place. The ghosts.

For here on the walls were the outlines of the Mountainfolk, the people of whom his grandfather had spoken. Here, too, were the mountain peaks and the rocky pillars, and the carved ice-coracles in a swelling sea of cloud The images of the Mountainfolk were faded now, some scarcely visible through centuries of water stain and green-black lichen scabs. Painted in burnt oranges and reds, grainy as a sepia photograph, the men were lithe and muscular, heavily bearded against the savage cold. And, amongst them, the womenfolk. Thin-boned and pale.

He thought again of the story old Helygen had told, and

saw the people on these walls with new eyes. For the first time, he recognized them as the very same people in the picture at home.

He looked about him.

Could it be that these Mountainfolk were not just myth, but had truly lived here, where the air was thin? And had they told their story in these paintings before climbing upwards and sailing from the polluted, poisonous air?

He looked more closely than before, with older eyes.

His brow furrowed.

Licking a finger, he drew it across an image, bringing its colours to life, the women dancing in the candlelight.

And now his heart raced. There was something ... something new... But what?

A shiver broke Sundeep's reverie, and he glanced down. His cup was empty and the cold was sucking at the marrow of his bones. It was time to go.

Pinching the wick, he left the candle and felt his way out once more into the Bowl. Pausing long enough for his eyes to become accustomed to the starlight, he glanced back; and his heart lurched. For now he knew.

It wasn't the images of a lost life that had captivated him as a child, and which had done so once again. Nor was it the story each rock told, nor the presence of the past in the now. Not the delicacy of the paintings. Not the familiarity of the place.

No.

It was the womenfolk.

For in their gold-splashed eyes, their sunrise hair, their light frames and the pallor of their skin, was recognition.

He had seen his mother.

When Meirwen climbed from this place, she had been going home.

※

The Stairway

*

SUNDEEP MOVED IN THE STARLIGHT, down a confusion of narrow paths which branched, twisted and turned back upon themselves. It was almost impossible to maintain any sense of direction, and an intruder might easily lose himself amongst the great boulders. The only way to get out was to know the route by heart and to follow the crystals in the wall, which at any crucial junction would sparkle to mark the way. In the past, Sundeep had always been with his mother, who could walk the route with her eyes shut, laughing all the while. For him, it was not so easy, and he had occasionally to scale a large rock to get his bearings.

But his steps proved sure, and led at last to a small oval chamber where the rock walls hung like the folds of gigantic black drapes. Sundeep walked to the centre, and paused.

A fraction of a moment later, he had gone.

The way out had been concealed – the rock wall seemed solid when viewed face-on. Even if you walked around the whole chamber, it was impossible to detect the gap until you were right upon it. For the face was composed of not one, but two, layers. The rock arced smoothly from the left, then without warning dropped back a foot or so before continuing its sweep. Just at this point, the giant folds of the right-hand wall stopped abruptly. The result was a narrow entrance, but wide enough for a man to squeeze into.

Until now, Sundeep had always stopped at this point, watching as his mother slipped away. Now he hesitated, breathed deeply, then continued.

He was surprised by the narrowness of the passage and the smoothness of its walls and floor. There was just enough space to edge along sideways, head to one side, pack held ahead in outstretched hand; but not enough to draw a deep breath. Just before he began to panic, he came out at the base of what appeared to be a stairway. For here, in the heart of the Mountain, was a huge split, a rising ramp, its massive walls soaring a thousand feet to the stars. From its foot, a cascade of rockfall rose upwards. And in its midst, a zigzag pathway of stones snaked ahead.

Sundeep started out, amazed to find that the fallen stones were in fact a careful construct of steps – in every case the surface of one rock rose no more than eight inches above the last. But the going was hard, for the altitude was beginning to tell. He imagined his mother skipping up these stones with a song, seeming to draw strength from every upward step, while his father had struggled to reach even the Secret Place below. Sundeep had always kept his mother's pace, but now movement demanded deeper breaths.

He slowed as the air thinned, and softly counted out each step.

One-and-two-and-three-and-four.

Steady now.

Slow and steady.

After each hundred steps, he paused to rest, leaning

forwards with his hands on his thighs until his breathing settled.

Now and then he met a fallen boulder that choked the passage. Sometimes, he could wriggle under it. More often, he was forced to scale it, leaving him gasping for breath at the top.

And with the altitude came the cold. The damp surface of the rocks hardened into a thin casing of ice. More than once he lurched downwards, his grip failing him.

Minutes turned to hours, and all the while the air thinned and cooled.

Below, the walls of the crack converged, like a ladder dropping into the mouth of a well.

Onwards.

Silence.

Almost imperceptibly, the height of the walls reduced, and the angle eased until the crack was no more than a shallow wedge.

Shuffling and panting, he stumbled the final two hundred yards out onto the snow.

Sundeep had climbed from deep valley to high mountain, from high summer to deep winter. Even the snow was unfamiliar. Below, when it came, the snow was soft and light as down. Here it was coarse and stale, beaten by high-altitude winds, baked by sun and frozen by night.

He was standing in a deep V-shaped gully. Ahead, set into the facing wall, was a disc of ice, its surface a frosted mirror. Trickles of now-frozen meltwater channelled across its surface. To his left, the path in the gulley floor wound out of sight behind a rocky pillar. Strapping his crampons to his boots, Sundeep took an ice-axe in each hand and stepped forward, snow chips scurrying from his feet. He moved cautiously, testing the crampon bite, sure that he would at any moment slip. He had gone not five yards when he stopped in awe.

Ahead, a huge icy ledge clung to the side of the Mountain, drenched in a century of snow. Thousands of feet below he could just make out his tiny home, the smoke from the dying fire a flat trace from the chimney. At the far end of the valley range upon range of distant mountains faded from view; a rocky pinnacle marked the end of the ledge, beyond which layers of peaks were beginning to appear.

But to the right, more awesome still, was a vast cathedral

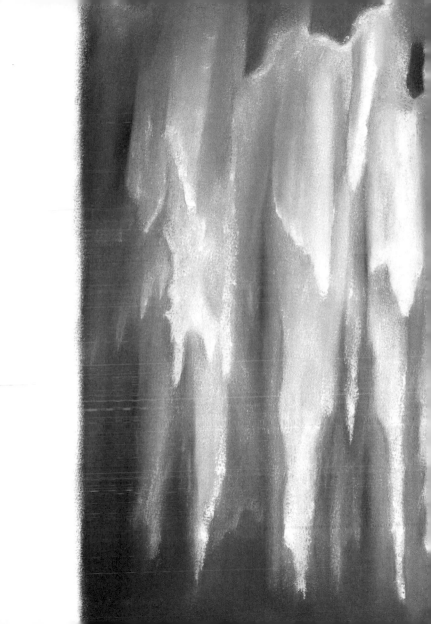

of soaring steeples, columns and spires, sculpted in stone and ice – every surface lacquered and crusted, powdered and dusted, in the whitest of snows. In the middle, a massive bowl; a hanging hall of marble white, pierced by a simple standing stone dressed in winter rime. Leading from it, a series of lonely rock pillars swept upwards to a wall of thick blue ice.

And as he stood, the trickle of time thickened slowly in the cold, until it ceased to flow at all.

How his mother must have marvelled at this place.

Yet this was not the end. Not where his mother would have stopped, nor where she would have died. For Sundeep recognized this place from the picture above the cottage fire. He had ascended the bouldered Stairway, and stood now upon the hanging Ledge. To his right he recognized the near-vertical face of frozen blue water.

He knew to go on – towards the great Ice-Wall.

✳

The Ice-Wall

SUNDEEP MOVED SWIFTLY across the apple-crisp snow of the Ledge. The moon was high, and the face ahead suffused with cold light. He could feel his breath quickening as he approached the slope, hear the snow slab creaking beneath his weight.

The angle steepened, and he kicked in hard, winnowing ice-grains from the ground.

Kick. Step. Kick. Step. Breath, breath, breath, breath.

The slope steepened, its surface rising to meet him. Leaning inwards, he sought support, stabbing his axe handles into the skin of the Mountain with each step, sinking the long wooden shafts into the white snow beneath.

Kick. Step. Breath. Breath.

The rhythm changed as he gained height and the air grew thinner. Below, the Cathedral and the Bowl began to recede. Almost imperceptibly, the snow slope had given way to the wall of solid blue ice.

Kick. Breath. Step. Breath.

He was working harder now.

And now he could no longer walk, but was forced to climb, standing near-upright.

Swing the axe.

Take the weight.

Kick in the front points of the crampons.

Breathe. Breathe.

Step up. Pause.

Onwards.

Minutes. Hours?

His throat was dry.

Swing. Secure. Pause.

Kick. Climb. Pause.

His brow leaked sweat.

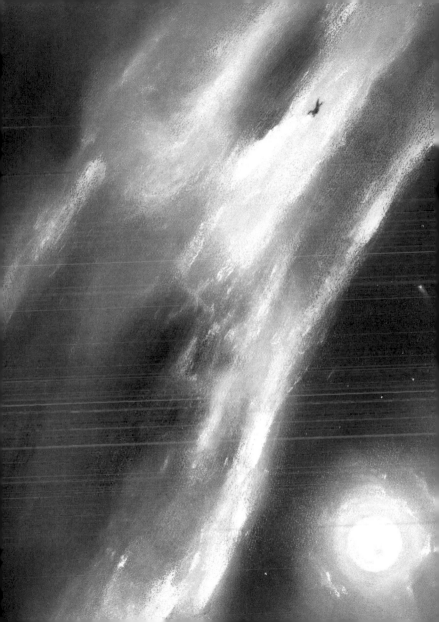

Panting

Heavily

From

Exertion.

The air was too thin to feel, but he could taste its cold metal.

Swing. Secure. Pause.

Kick. Climb. Pause.

Only rarely did he look down, and when he did his chest tightened with fear. His steps released a tinkling cascade of ice-diamonds. With each axe-stroke, larger shards were launched into freefall, floating outwards in gentle arcs before accelerating and slicing into the slope below, where they left linear footprints as they bounded across the snow, the clatter echoing around the vast ampitheatre.

Swing. Secure. Pause. Kick. Climb. Pause.

Swing. Secure. Pause. Kick. Climb. Pause.

Breath rasping.

Fingers numbed and locked.

But then, almost without warning, the pitch began to level. He was leaning forwards to plant his axe, taking his weight on all fours, more crawling than standing. And, finally he *could* stand.

Then,

Legs disowned,

Staggered

Slowly.

Heaving for

Breath.

Out. Onto. The

Col

Itself.

He stood: desperately panting, eyes bulging, hungry for air.

But there was none.

He had come too far, too fast. He knew it now.

His clothing was frozen, his gloves as much ice as wool.

Around him, a blanket of clouds had risen to the shoulder of the Ice-Wall.

The air pained him with cold, sanding his skin, hooking his lungs at every breath. He fumbled the thick scarf across his mouth, but the dampness gelled it to his nose and lips.

He stood, mind and body paralysed.

What now?

He felt faint.

Everything was speeding away from him, was becoming distant.

And he was hallucinating. For there, beached beside a pinnacle, lay a coracle of ice, its gossamer sail half-furled and filled with starlight.

He turned. The world revolved slowly around him. Very slowly. Blurring.

Behind, the Ice-Wall. No retreat.

To the left and right, the Mountain fell steeply away.

Ahead, a sloping cliff face as black as the night. Above it, a huge wave of ice clinging to the edge of the rock. And above that, a ramp of ever-thinning air, leading upwards to a gasping gaping nothingness.

Sundeep sank to his knees, his forehead pressed against the snow, gulping and mouthing silent Os.

His life was leaving him. He could feel it.

He gently sagged, the black sky racing in to envelop him as he lost consciousness.

※

The Old Man
& the Girl

THERE WAS SMOKE IN THE AIR.

Burning. Choking.

Couldn't breathe.

House on fire!

Sundeep struggled to sit.

"Hush, now, valley boy. There's little enough air for you here, and what there is should not be wasted."

The voice was a summer river, warm and deep, its bed rough gravel. A hand pressed gently on his shoulder, and another on his forehead.

Sundeep settled back on his elbows and opened his eyes.

He seemed to be in a cave of some sort. At the rear, a small fire flickered, the smoke drawn into a chimney cut into the roof above. On the wall hung a large brown scimitar, its blade gleaming in the light of the flames, curved and pointed and razor-edged. Beside it was a sharp white pick of similar size, ending in a needlepoint.

Sundeep blinked and looked again, for here were the "gifts of tooth and claw" which rested above the fireplace in his own cottage far below.

Nearby, something moved swiftly into the shadows.

He tried to focus in the half-light, but could not. He turned back his gaze.

Beside him crouched a man; an old man, weary and wise. His eyes were of molten brass, the lids red in their glow. His old leather skin was laced with a million creases, and his hair and beard were frosted grass.

The man proffered a shallow wooden bowl. The hand that held it was covered in coarse hair, the joints gnarled and fused.

"Drink."

The brew was bitter and dark, strong with the flavours of

moss and bark and berry. Yet it was comforting, and Sundeep's breathing began to settle. The old man smiled.

"At last we meet. An old man welcomes you."

He gestured slowly behind him. "And so, too, does Morchilla."

From the shadows around the fire, she appeared; slight but strong and very, very beautiful. Her eyes threw frightened flames of gold, and his heart leapt for her, as he recognized, somewhere within, a sorrow.

The old man coughed suddenly, eyelids clenched in pain, forehead furrowed, as he raised a fist to his chest. Morchilla looked anxious, and took a step towards him, but he waved her away with his hand.

When he had recovered his breath, Sundeep spoke.

"Who are you?" He looked around him. "And how did I come to be here?"

The old man smiled.

"Forgive me. Although your questions will be answered, there is little time, for the sun will rise and the slopes weaken. If you do not leave, you will be taken from us as were those before you."

"But…"

The old man raised his hand. "In good time." He smiled. "There is much that you would know. So let me begin." He seated himself cross-legged, his arm around Morchilla, and began.

"You may have been told the story of the Mountainfolk, for many children hear the tale. Most Lowlanders think it a myth, a fairy tale, a fable embellished over the centuries. For them, the Mountainfolk are not, and never were.

"But perhaps, for you, it is more than myth, for you have seen the Secret Place – as did your parents – and know it to be real. You have seen the paintings on the walls. For you, the Mountainfolk are not – but perhaps once were. But the truth is this: the Mountainfolk were, and still *are*. And on this mountain, we" – his gesture swept from himself to the girl – "are all that remain, although others live amongst the distant ranges."

He paused, allowing his breathing to settle. Then he nodded and continued, with sadness in his voice.

He told of the fragile beauty of the Earth when she was young, and of how blessed were the Menfolk. How some came to dwell upon the high ground, adapting to the cold thin air, whilst others settled in the valleys and slowly lost their ability to ascend. And how, with time, the Mountainfolk were forgotten by the Lowlanders.

"Once this mountain was dense with Mountainfolk who dwelled in caves on all sides. Some descended to forage at night, others remained. And, with claw and tooth of the yeti" – he gestured to the objects hung upon the wall – "they sculpted coracles from the very ice. Long before dawn, whole fleets of ice-ships would be moored to the nearby pinnacles, bobbing on the clouds, ready to ferry food and fuel around the Mountain."

The old man gazed far ahead at the distant memory.

"Such beauty." He shook his head. "A thousand craft moored in the Cathedral below, or even here if the cloud was high; hidden from the sight of the Lowlanders by the vapour upon which they floated. And in the moonlight, they sparkled like jewels, clinking against one another like wind-chimes. Once loaded, they would settle on their sea, then glide ahead propelled by silent paddles which left curls of cloud in their wake."

He frowned. "But by dawn the folk retreated, for they did not dare be seen. And these were dangerous seas on which to sail, for the rising sun would make them boil and rage, tearing great gaps in the clouds and leaving nothing but the clear blue skies of dawn."

Morchilla rose, gathered their wooden bowls and filled them from the pot above the fire. Sundeep watched her; observed her strength and grace. The gentle touch upon the old man's shoulder, and their warm shared smiles.

When she was done, the girl sat beside them and glanced at the old man, who nodded to her to take up the tale.

"One night, in the depths of winter and darkness, a Mountainman descended. His name was Ptarmagon, and he moved swiftly from the heights, dropping down the Spiral to exit beneath the great Wall of Ice. He paused briefly beside the Ledge, then stepped lightly down the Stairway and into the Secret Place.

"He emerged onto the hillside high above the home-steads, the strong winds gusting about him, whipping thin trails of snow across his face. He wrapped his furs more closely about him and continued downwards on iron soil, crossing the frozen land in search of wolf and fox, of food from the stores of those who dwelled below.

"Foraging in the valley, he approached a small wooden house through an orchard of olive trees, and glanced inside. And there he saw Awelan, sleeping and beautiful. Her flesh was white as ice; her face as calm as the midnight hour, as bright as a settled star; and her slow breath was a fountain of frosted diamonds in the cold air. She felt his gaze upon her and awoke, finding a strange but handsome man before her, smiling and unmoving."

As the girl spoke, the old man's face filled with joy, yet ached with loss.

"You remember this man?" Sundeep asked.

The old man turned to him, his eyes distant as he spoke. "Yes indeed, young Sundeep. All this is as yesterday to me. For that Mountainman was me. I am Ptarmagon. And I was blessed. For Awelan awoke and fell in love with me, as I had with her; something which a coarse man of the mountains never did deserve.

"We courted in secret. Awelan would slip silently from her room at night as I descended from the mountains to meet her amongst the white-crusted trees of the grove. But our time together was brief, for I would always return before dawn. Finally, however, we could keep our secret no longer, and were married not one year later, her family never suspecting whence this stranger" – he gestured to himself – "had come. The secret of the Mountainfolk was ours alone.

"We made our home partway up the mountainside, where the air was thin enough for my health, yet of sufficient richness for the comfort of my wife. And on occasion, when certain that we could not be seen, we would go up to the Secret Place. She would sit amongst the Mountainfolk who still dwelled there, the only Lowlander to know of their existence, while I ascended further, through the Crack and up the Stairway, across the frozen Ledge and through the Cathedral, climbing the great Ice-Wall to visit my family high, high above.

"Nine months passed, and Awelan bore us the most beautiful of daughters. This daughter grew healthy and strong and happy, equally at ease in the rich heavy air of the valley and the gasping vacuum of the upper mountain slopes.

"By now, the lowland air was foul and bitter as never

before, and my people could descend only briefly, I tried my best to help my kin high above. Masked by nightfall, Awelan and I would journey with our daughter to the Secret Place, carrying packs of wood and wine and such foodstuffs as we could spare. Our daughter had inherited my capacity to survive in the thin air, and from here she would shoulder her share of the load and climb onwards with me to the Mountainfolk, bounding from rock to rock, racing the snow from a slope whilst Awelan waited patiently for our return.

"The years passed, and our daughter became a woman; a beautiful woman, full of joy and laughter, now betrothed to a Lowlander. But all the while I was weakening, for the Lowlanders had grown in number, their cities consuming all around them, their factories polluting the very air we breathed. And I found myself slowly poisoned, until the day came when I could stay no longer. But how could I leave? I would rather die than abandon the wife and daughter I loved so dearly. I would not go."

Sundeep looked puzzled. "But you live here, high upon the Mountain." He looked around. "What became of your wife?"

Ptarmagon's head lowered. "Awelan loved me very much.

She could not bear to see me suffer as the lowland air sickened me day after day."

His voice was thick with sadness. "And so it was that the sacrifice was made."

He sighed, then drew breath.

"Perhaps she administered a sleeping draught, for I have more dreams than memories of that fateful night. In the midst of that winter, when the roaring gales charged at the walls and battered the timber frame, while the avalanches exploded far above, while lightning flashed and snow shrapnelled all around, Awelan slipped from our bed, kissing my fingers as tears spilled silently down her cheeks. She paused at our daughter's side, drew a finger across her cheek, and left a smear upon the sleeping girl's brow.

"And with that, Awelan walked from the house and out into the harsh night, to die.

"My daughter and I were left alone."

The air was cooling as the fire died. Sundeep watched Morchilla rise to tend it. She glanced at the paltry pile of unburnt sticks which lay near by, but added no more to the hearth. With care, she raked the embers, turning the one remaining log until it crackled with flames once more.

Satisfied, she settled beside them, her hand upon old Ptarmagon's shoulder. Catching Sundeep's eyes upon her, the old man and the girl shared a smile.

Morchilla spoke, her voice steady and soft. "No. I am not the daughter." She looked at Ptarmagon, who nodded for her to continue.

"This mountain stands alone. No ridges or bridges of snow connect her to others. And when the clouds rise to encircle her, she is seen as she is: an island.

"No longer able to descend into the lowland air for food, we Mountainfolk could not survive. We hunted mountain fox and wolf and bear, using the skins for clothing and the flesh for food. But we could not take more than the Earth had to give – soon these creatures would all have been killed. So we began to gather lichen in the summers, using it for mattresses, as fuel for fires, as food in broth. But this was not enough, and the weak and sick began to die. Ptarmagon's daughter did her best for her father and his folk – for us – ferrying supplies beyond the Secret Place, her own husband

and son now waiting for her to return. But even this could not suffice.

"And so a council was called, and it was decided: a fleet of coracles would be built, and those who could, would leave, sailing the ocean cloud to the distant ranges far to the north and west." She waved her arm in a broad sweep. "There, the air was pure and the valleys fertile, and life could begin again.

"The coracles were carved and paddles made and once prepared, we waited. Waited for the time to be right, as no such journey had ever before been attempted, no voyages made from range to range.

"At last, the weather was stable and kind. The days grew warm, the nights clear and cold, and dense cloud rose from the Lowlands to lap their shores as evening fell. The boats were loaded with provisions, and the Mountainfolk made ready. And then, one night, they launched their ships."

Ptarmagon resumed the tale, sadness in his voice. "I watched them as they went, the menfolk making firm strokes with their paddles. And the cloud glowed bright behind them in their wake.

"But soon the men began to tire. Higher cloud appeared, weakening the light of the moon, and the sails began to sag. Their progress slowed.

"By dawn they had almost reached the distant range. Other Mountainfolk appeared along the lower crests and ridges to welcome their kin. Some of the voyagers made landfall, casting lines ashore and landing their passengers safely. But most lagged behind, their crews exhausted and weak with exertion. Yet, terrified by the approach of dawn and their passengers' pleas, they struggled on.

"But then, quite suddenly, it was too late. The sun began to rise, and the white cloud seas to boil. Columns of cloud erupted about them, the coracles rocking violently as the travellers were flung from their capsizing craft. There was nothing we could do." He shook his head. "And in the valley far below, Ptarmagon's daughter had watched through the night, hoping for a glimpse of the boats above. She wept as the fragile flecks of ice slipped silently from their stormy sea and plunged to earth, a shower of falling stars in the glow of the early sun."

*

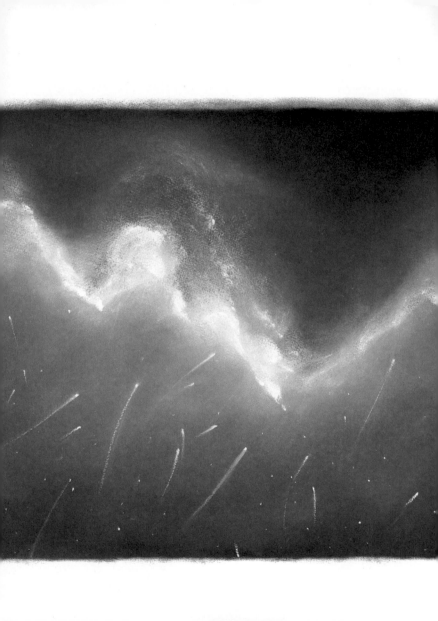

The old man tugged at his matted hair and a spate of coughing wracked his frail body. It was some minutes before he could speak again. Rising from the floor, he walked to the cave entrance and frowned.

"We have but moments before the sun rises. You must leave at once. Fortunately, your descent will be faster than your climb, but still you must go."

Sundeep stood, finding that his legs were no longer weak, and that he breathed more easily. He smiled as the old man eyed him.

"The brew has assisted you. But even so, you have something of the strength of a Mountainman." He turned. "Come."

Sundeep took a single step before glancing back at the girl. Her eyes shone with the same tigerfire as those of his mother. She was slender and silent, compact and composed, and filled with loneliness. Somehow Sundeep understood her, and his heart ached inexplicably.

The old man was waiting at the mouth of the cave, but Sundeep turned from him and strode back across the room. He reached forward to Morchilla, held her hands and her gaze, then leaned in close to kiss her softly upon the cheek.

He followed the old man out of the cave and did not look back.

✳

Those Who Remained

THEY EMERGED onto a rocky ledge high among the cliffs, a vantage point from which the whole valley could be seen. The old man pulled his skins close around him. Looking down, Sundeep could make out the Ice-Wall and the Cathedral and, far below, the outline of his house.

The old man had been right. To the east, the sky was lightening.

He turned to find that the old man was already edging along the outside of his cave, the rough rock path but a foot or so wide, suspended dizzily above the crest. Following, Sundeep found that the path continued in among the crags, doubling back to cut through the icy cornice and zigzagging steeply down across the face of the cliff. They crossed the Saddle to the top of the Ice-Wall, where the old man stopped abruptly. The rock to their left was flattened, its lip forming what appeared to be a well.

"This is where we must part. Go safely, young Sundeep. Go safe and well."

Sundeep froze. "You know my name."

The old man shrugged.

There was a silence while Sundeep thought.

"You knew that I had visited the Secret Place. And you spoke, too, of my parents."

The old man nodded.

"How is it that you know me? And what do you know of my parents?"

The old man shook his head. "Not now, young Sundeep. But one day."

Sundeep looked him in the eye.

"Those were my mother's words, but now she is gone."

The old man glanced again at the gathering glow of dawn, and then at Sundeep. He sighed.

"I will begin, but the tale is long, and not one that I can yet complete. You must return to hear the conclusion."

He looked again to the east, where white was leeching into the sky.

"On that night – the night of the great exodus – when the coracle fleet slipped its moorings and later slid to Earth, it carried with it almost all who had once dwelled upon this mountain. Only three of us stayed behind – myself, an old widow and the orphan girl, Morchilla. Morchilla was too young and sickly to consider the crossing, and the old widow had agreed to remain with me, as her guardians. We were to follow later, when her strength was greater. I would sail them both across before returning to be near my beloved daughter.

"My daughter had grown to be as beautiful as Awelan, her mother. She lived below in the valley – was married now, and had borne a son. But, still, she did not forget her father. Each week she would climb with provisions; wood for the fire, meat and vegetables for the table, and occasionally wine to warm them. There was little enough to share, but the old widow and I needed less than Morchilla, who was growing strong.

"One fierce winter, a storm arose. But this was no ordinary storm. Tethered in the far west, it growled and snarled and howled until finally breaking free. It leapt loose and roared through the valleys, setting upon the Mountain. Days turned to weeks, and still the storm was not spent. The snows built deep upon the slopes, and we huddled in our cave as our stores diminished and our fire slowly died. And with it, our hope.

"Far below, not one person in the valley could remember such a storm. They listened as it bellowed in fury, snapping bolts of lightning this way and that, tearing rock from the cliffs and releasing massive slabs of ice. Glad of their stout timber dwellings, the Lowlanders kept indoors and fed their fires, secure in the knowledge that their stores would see them through.

"But one amongst them had other concerns. Each morning, my daughter would gaze to the west for some sign that the storm was weakening. But there was no such sign. Her days were spent staring towards the lost Mountain, its peaks hidden in the swirling whiteness, where she knew us to be starving, slowly failing in the cold.

She was determined that we must be helped.

"Her husband insisted that she should not go. The storm would hunt her down, and then four would be dead instead of three, and her son would be motherless.

"My daughter was tormented, her dreams a confusion of snow and suffering, until finally she could bear it no more. She got up one morning and gathered kindling and logs, oil and olives, vegetables and cheese, dried meats, dates and figs. Her husband helped her sadly but silently, for he knew that she had made her decision. The packs she carried were heavy, for those above had had no provisions for some weeks now, and there was no telling how much longer the storm would rage.

"She kissed her sleeping son and husband. 'Do not fear for me.' The door closed behind her. Head down, she struggled out into the blizzard."

And here, the old man ceased his tale, and looked anxiously eastwards.

"It is time for you to leave, young Sundeep, for the sun is rising. The Lowlanders must not see you come down the Mountain. None remain who know of our existence, nor do we wish them to."

Sundeep shook his head.

"But you have not yet finished your story. What has this to do with me? With my family?"

The old man smiled.

"Return soon, young orphan. Bring with you food for fire and flame, and for our mortal hunger; for we have little left to eat. Return, and the tale shall be completed. And in it you shall find your answer."

"But how can I return? The air here is far too thin – without you, I would have died."

"And so a debt is partly paid."

He paused.

"Have no fear. You have a little of the blood of the Mountainfolk in your veins. Your next ascent will prove easier, as will each of those that follows."

He raised a single finger.

"But mark my words, there is danger in such enterprise. Those whose blood is mixed of mountain and lowland must be wary. Dwell in the high mountains too long, and you will be denied return to the valleys, where the air will prove too rich and too poisonous. Stay too long, and you shall stay for ever."

The old man tugged gently at Sundeep's sleeve.

"Come."

He guided Sundeep to sit on the lip of the well, and put his pack on his lap.

"Now go. And return to learn the answers you seek."

The push was sudden and unexpected. And with it, the boy was gone, falling into the neck of the well.

Sundeep yelped as he slipped suddenly into the blackness. He seemed to drop vertically for perhaps only a few feet before finding himself in a narrow tunnel, its floor as smooth as an oiled whetstone.

He was lying on his back, sliding ever faster, the straps and buckles of his pack jangling and whistling as he skittered and skimmed through the middle of the Mountain.

He had no control.

His chest was tight with fear, his breath coming in snatches.

Light flashed across him from his right, through slots carved in the outer surface of the Spiral, more for ventilation than view.

He tried to see. Hugging the pack to his belly, he bent at the waist, then crashed back down as his forehead grazed the rock roof.

Helter-skelter he continued, dizzied by the descent.

A mounting pressure against his back told him that, at last, the slide was levelling. Suddenly a bright disc of frosted light appeared ahead and the ice shattered as his feet struck its centre. And with that, he was launched from the tunnel mouth, out onto a bed of hardened snow.

Sundeep lay winded and confused, staring upwards at a lightening sky for some moments before slowly rising to his feet and dusting himself down. Looking about, he found to his astonishment that he was at the corner of the Ledge, just at the junction where it met the gully from the Crack. The porthole of ice through which he had crashed lay splintered all around. But already the warmth of the morning rays was causing meltwater to trickle over it; the opening would once more freeze over as night fell.

Sundeep skirted the gully and descended into the Crack, moving swiftly from step to step, sliding beneath this boulder and that, and dropping as softly as a snow leopard from the heights. Within an hour, he had reached the Secret Place. He was about to duck into the shelter to retrieve his candle when he stopped.

He would leave it where it was.

For he would return.

✳

The Return

✳

SUNDEEP SLEPT through much of the next day, exhausted by the severity of the climb and the emotions of the night. And when he woke, the emptiness and cold of night and heart had gone. In their place was a fullness of light.

He got up and went outside. Sheltering his eyes against the sun, he looked up at the Mountain, following the winding path to his right. High above and to the left, he could make out the Ledge. To its right would be the portal and the exit from the Crack. Beyond this lay the Cathedral and, towering vertically above it, the blue smear of the Ice-Wall.

He followed it up to the Saddle, straining his eyes to see the rock cliff and the hanging cornice above. Just to the right lay a black speck of rock. Here, he knew, were the old man and Morchilla. His new friends.

He raised his arms over his head and waved them slowly, letting those above know that he would not abandon them.

He walked to the small timber shed, took the shears and made his way to the olive grove, where he trimmed the trees and vines in turn. And as he worked, he settled to the rhythm of the shears, absorbed in the scent of the soil and colours of the ripening fruit. Life had joy once more.

That night he lit his fire and was about to go to bed when suddenly he paused, then stepped outside. Ahead, the Mountain towered black and featureless. Above it stars teemed and crowded, spitting and crackling as the cold night drew breath. Against the skyline, a thin trace of smoke rose into the blackness. And he thought of those above. Of Ptarmagon. And of Morchilla.

He thought especially of Morchilla.

Sundeep rested further on the following day, gathering crops in the morning, and spending the afternoon in sleep. He rose early in the evening, however, and made ready to climb the Mountain again. This time his pack would be crammed with cheese and meat and vegetables, olives and apricots. And to his load, he added his grandfather's old pipe and his mother's small perfume bottle. As the moon drifted slowly upwards, he set out once more. Despite the weight he carried, his steps seemed stronger, his soles skimming light across the soil, his feet flitting from stone to stone as the Mountain drew him ever upwards.

He reached the Secret Place, lit his candle and rested under the sloping stone, leaning comfortably against his pack. Then, his sweet tea drained, he followed the path, the crystals winking amongst the rocks.

This time his steps were sure, and in a matter of minutes he was slipping around the veil of rock to reappear at the base of the Crack. He looked up along its vast length, remembering his struggles with the thinning air not two days earlier. But this time was different. His feet danced up the steps, and he slid easily under fallen boulders. When he climbed, his grip was strong, his breathing slow and steady;

and he heard his mother's voice, singing the Song of the Valley.

Leaving the Stairway and approaching the Ledge, he looked to his right and smiled. The portal had already frozen over again, thin ice sealing the exit from the Spiral. He stopped to kick his crampons repeatedly into the ground, scraping together a softer mattress of snow on which to land when he returned.

The Ledge was beautiful and silent, the valley beneath framed in black rock and glazed with clear air. Behind it, the Cathedral spires soared and spiked the sky, the frosted rock flutes muffling the sounds of his steps across the crisp snow of the Bowl.

On the Ice-Wall, his footholds were still where he had carved them – he had only to sweep them free of snow to step securely upon them. True, he dug harder with the points of his axes as the weight of his pack pulled him backwards, but the climb itself was easier. As the angle levelled to the slope of the col, he found himself almost sprinting with joy before kneeling to suck upon a handful of fresh white snow.

Sundeep was changing.

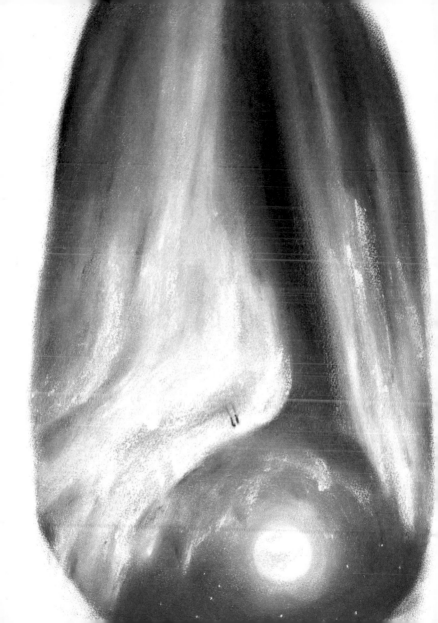

It was surely too early for Morchilla and Ptarmagon to be up, for Sundeep had made faster time than he could ever have believed possible. His eyes followed the thin path across the rockface through the cornice, to the rocky outcrop perhaps three hundred feet above. And here his heart leapt for, wrapped in a fur and crouched low for warmth, sat Morchilla. She had been waiting for him.

As he began to climb, he saw her retreat into the cave. The charcoal trace of smoke from the rocks high above thickened to a broad brushstroke as the fire was stoked. It was spitting with flame as he reached the cave. Morchilla turned briefly to smile at him, her gaze falling fast to the floor as she tended a pot of water.

From his corner bed, the old man rose, shuffling forwards with bent back and stiffened joints to greet him.

He opened his arms. "You have returned."

He was more breathless, and his eyes seemed weaker than before.

He coughed.

Together they unloaded the pack, laying out the contents

upon the stone floor. The old man smiled as he was handed the pipe.

"I cannot think that time will allow me much use of this, but I thank you, young Sundeep."

Sundeep turned to Morchilla. "From my mother." Then he shook his head. "From me. It was my mother's." He gave her the small perfume bottle and she blushed momentarily as their fingers met.

They ate well together. The old man and Morchilla were no longer fearful of starvation, for they knew Sundeep would return again. As they settled down to drink the warming brew of herbs and berries, Sundeep turned to the old man.

"You said you would complete your tale."

Ptarmagon packed his pipe, sweet tobacco now mixed with the lichen in the bowl. "I did." He made no effort to continue.

Sundeep prompted him. "The Mountainfolk were caught in a storm. Your daughter was bringing food and drink to you and your companions."

The old man nodded, took a twig from the fire and held its glowing tip over the bowl of his pipe.

"Please. You must go on. What has this to do with my mother? With my parents? How is it that you knew me?"

Ptarmagon drew on his pipe. "In good time, my boy. In good time."

He settled back upon one elbow and turned his head to face Sundeep.

His voice was soft and tired, and burdened with memory.

"High in the Mountain, the orphan girl, the old widow and I were slowly weakening, and all around the storm raged. Below, my daughter bade her husband farewell and put on her pack, determined to save us. She stepped out into the blizzard, back bent under her burden, knees buckling with each step. She thought of how Awelan, her mother, had chosen to die in such a storm.

"The path to the Secret Place was waist-deep in snow, through which she waded as if crossing a cold mountain river. A tormenting wind snatched at her clothes, hurling handfuls of ice sharp against her face. A white rim of frost formed rapidly around her eyes and icicles cascaded from the cloth covering her mouth. And yet still she went on."

Ptarmagon tried to stifle a cough, but was seized by it.

Morchilla patted him gently on the back, taking up the tale as his breathing settled. Her voice was as soft and sweet as honey. As she spoke, Sundeep studied her more closely. She did indeed have the rust-flecked eyes of his mother. The same clear white complexion, too.

"Buried deep within the Mountain and shielded from the savagery of the storm, the Secret Place offered some respite. Here the woman rested briefly, then struggled on through the Crack, her load straining against her back, the straps cutting deep into her shoulders, soaked by melting snow from without and by sweat from within. But still she climbed.

"She pulled herself up the Stairway, cascades of powder hissing from above and filling the cracks and crevices of her clothing. She hauled herself over ice-smeared boulders, slipping again and again until her knees were bruised and bloodied. Her hands were freezing, her fingers white. But never did she falter.

"She reached the Ledge, which burgeoned with snow. The Snow Bowl echoed to crack and rumble from above. The Cathedral was in chaos, littered with deep debris from the avalanches, which spewed in torrential waterfall over the lip of the Ice-Wall. But still she advanced, scraping snow from the ice and planting each axe in turn. There came a roar from above, and she pressed herself flat into the face of the Mountain, a plume of white engulfing her and almost sweeping her from her holds. But even then she climbed on."

Morchilla rose, and absent-mindedly began to pace the cave. She picked up the small perfume bottle Sundeep had given her, and a smile began to form on her face, but was eclipsed by a frown. She came back to sit with them, holding the perfume bottle.

"Deep in the cave we sat, huddled together for warmth as the embers of the fire glowed their last. And here she found us, slumped and still, as cold as death itself. Despite her own exhaustion, she would not rest, reviving the fire with fresh timbers, and our flesh with hot broth."

There were tears in Morchilla's eyes. Her voice faltered.

"And we were saved."

The old man looked towards her and waited, then took up the tale once more. "Outside, the storm thrashed and lashed at the cave, howling and pawing at the entrance. I begged my daughter not to face its wrath, to remain with us. And so she did for two days, hoping that the wind would subside.

"On the third day, she left. She was of mixed blood, and if she stayed longer risked never being able to return to her husband and son below.

"We watched as she skirted the narrow ledge, buffeted by the raging wind. Watched as she pushed on through the cornice and followed the zigzag path across the black cliff face.

"Reaching the Saddle, she pushed on towards the entrance to the Spiral and paused, turning to smile at us above. And then she heard it. A portentous creak. A moan, a crack. And then a screech like tortured metal. The cornice – the wave of frozen ice which hung above – had broken free beneath its burden of snow.

"She ran as never before, hurling herself headlong towards the Spiral, driven by fear and love for her son and husband; and had almost reached it when the tumult was upon her – a million tons of snow falling like foaming surf; tossing her, battering her, burying her, and sweeping her in a relentless torrent beyond the lip of the Ice-Wall.

"And so it was that my daughter gave her life for me, as her mother Awelan had before her."

✴

The Third Sacrifice

PTARMAGON DREW ON HIS PIPE, savouring the smouldering mixture. But then he coughed once more, raised a clenched fist and tapped it hard against the centre of his chest.

When the coughing had settled, they sat together in silence, the perfume bottle between them. The old man smiled, and spoke.

"That was the last storm of winter. The provisions my daughter had brought were sufficient for the coming weeks, after which the weather would get warmer. Below, the son wept at the loss of his mother, and her husband was consumed with sorrow, guilt and rage. How could he have let her go? Why had he not done more to dissuade her? He was responsible. She had died because of him. But those who lived high amongst the Mountains were also to blame. His wife had been nothing but a beast of burden to them, a mule to bring them food.

"For some months, he took food to the Secret Place, leaving it on the lower parts of the Stairway for us to collect, not wanting to face those he held responsible for the death of his wife.

"As I grew older, the descent became more arduous and my body found it ever harder to cope with the lowland air. But over the long summer months our stores were replenished.

"But the bitterness grew in the Lowlander's heart. They had killed his wife. They, too, should die. He would no longer carry provisions to the Secret Place. He would abandon them. Let them suffer as he was now suffering.

"And suffer we did."

Ptarmagon stopped and slowly shook his head, then resumed the tale.

"We knew at once that something was wrong, on the first

day the Lowlander failed to leave supplies. I had gone down through the Spiral and stumbled through the Crack, only to have to make the long ascent home empty-handed. The next week was the same, and the next. And all the while we looked down from our eyrie, watching the man, the boy and his grandfather tend their crops far below. As winter came again, our stores ran low. With little left but lichen, we knew that soon our time would come. The snows arrived once more, the days shortened, and the temperatures fell.

"But my daughter had chosen well: her husband was not an evil man. With time his pain ebbed, and in its place a new guilt arose. How could he honour the memory of his wife by allowing her father to die? His eyes began to drift to the mountains, and he once more prepared his pack and provisions.

"High on the Mountain I kept my vigil, and watched as he set out up the path. There was no time to waste. My strength all but gone, I stumbled from the Spiral, and reached the Secret Place just as he arrived.

"We wept and hugged each other. And he departed, promising to return the following night.

"And so he did. And continued to do for some time."

*

Ptarmagon rose and slowly paced the cave floor, his ageing joints stiff from cold and immobility. Walking to the cave mouth, Morchilla on his arm, he beckoned to Sundeep to join them. He stretched out an arm, pointing far into the distance. The clouds had settled in the valleys and all below was white, but far in the west, where white met black, a mountain range pushed upwards and breached the most distant horizon.

"There."

Sundeep craned his neck, straining to see what the old man meant. And then he saw it. The Mountain was alight with a hundred glow-worm flecks of orange, melting and retreating and flaring, distorted by the distance.

"Our people," said Morchilla. "When you go down, look far to your right, and you will see the full extent of the range. There are many mountains and many homes."

Sundeep nodded.

"Imagine the loneliness of being left behind, when our people, those we loved most, could be seen but not be touched." The old man coughed again, then shrugged. "Perhaps it matters less to those who know they are dying."

They returned to the fire and settled once more beside it as the old man coaxed his pipe to life.

Sundeep was puzzled. "Why did you not try to leave – the three of you?"

"The passage of time had changed us," Ptarmagon answered. "The old widow and I had become frail – life, for us, would be short. I wanted to live out my last days on the mountain of my birth, for below in the valley was all that remained of my family: Awelan, my wife, was dead; as was my daughter. My grandson, whom I had never met, was all that remained of my bloodline.

"The widow, however, longed to reach the distant ranges. She had done her duty in caring for Morchilla and yearned to leave. And Morchilla must go too. She had grown beautiful and strong, and she deserved a life filled with youth and laughter. If she stayed, she would be left alone after my death, condemned to a solitary life, trapped in this mountain prison.

"I knew they had to go. And yet I was too old and weak to take them myself.

"I spoke with the young Lowlander. I knew I had no right to ask for his help. He had already done so much, and had a

son for whom he must care. But the widow was sorrowful, and the orphan girl could not be left alone.

"The Lowlander knew what had to be done. He had abandoned us once, and would not do so again. There was but one choice – he would take them from this place.

"Never before had a Lowlander paddled one of the mountain ice-craft, and I was unsure that it would even take his weight, let alone that of two passengers. And so it was agreed that the Lowlander would sail the widow to her kin in the distant mountains, and then return for the orphan girl.

"Early one evening, he kissed his sleeping son goodbye and climbed briskly to this cave, by now more accustomed to the thin air. He reached the ledge outside just as the cloud rose and congealed in the cold night air. And through this slick of silver vapour, the distant mountains stood as islands.

"All day, I had carved an ice-coracle, larger and shallower than ever before so that it might support the weight of the Lowlander, and made beautiful in honour of its oarsman. Lapped by cloud and washed with moonlight, it bobbed gently on the ebb of rising air, clinking against the pinnacle to which it was moored. And as it did so, a million diamond facets fractured the starlight, scattering bright needles across the rockface."

"And did they succeed?" breathed Sundeep.

Ptarmagon did not answer directly. "The craft dipped as the Lowlander stepped aboard and settled. So low did it lie that wisps of cloud curled and trickled over its sides, baled out by the widow with wafts of her open hand.

"I slipped the line loose, and the coracle slid silently over the soft sea. As the Lowlander began to paddle with long slow sweeps, the widow turned towards us, her face wet with tears. Morchilla wept too, for she longed to join her people. But, if all went well, the Lowlander would soon return for her."

The old man slumped forwards, his eyes growing dim. Morchilla leaned close to him, knitting her fingers into his hair, and spoke, her voice low with sorrow.

"But it was not to be. The craft was too heavy, and waves of cloud crested its bow and spilled within. At first the old widow dispersed it with scooping movements of her hands. But with time she weakened and slowly the craft began to fill, settling lower and lower upon its sea. My son-in-law fought valiantly, alternating strokes of his blade with attempts to help her, but his Lowlander's body was exhausted by the exertion at such great height.

"They slowed and, as the sun began to rise, they knew that they would not survive. The Lowlander cradled the old widow's head on his shoulder and whispered comfort to her as the craft tilted and slipped out of view, a plume of vapour rising in its wake."

✳

Revelation

LATER THAT MORNING, Sundeep lay in the valley far below, cocooned in a blanket of warmed morning air. Outside, the bee was mumbling to itself among the peppers. The descent had been quicker than ever, and Sundeep was confident that future ascents would be equally speedy.

He tried to sleep, but found himself restless and unsettled. He had to return. Had to hear the end to Ptarmagon's tale. For soon – in only three days – he would be leaving for his new life on the coast.

He wandered barefoot into the orchard, pulling weeds and tending the soil, his mind adrift. And in this haze, the day passed slowly, lost in the heady scents of flower and fallen fruit.

At last the day was ending, the sun settling behind the western ridge, and Sundeep beneath his blankets, for he planned to rise early and set out once more to climb the Mountain.

And in the dark he lay there, his breath steady and strong, his eyes open, focused. And as he rested, he thought.

Thought about just how much had changed in these last days.

How much *he* had changed.

Of how much, too, he now knew – and had yet to learn. For much of what he had been told remained confusing. "You have a little of the blood of Mountainfolk within your veins," Ptarmagon had said. What did Ptarmagon mean by this? And how did Ptarmagon know of him and his parents?

And what *did* Sundeep know?

Little still, of his mother and father. But a great deal more of the Mountainfolk. Now he knew that the fairy tales were history.

That the myths were truth.

That the myths were true!

His breath faltered. Had his grandfather not spoken of the myth that is truth?

Just out of reach, a greater truth lay, like a word on the tip of a tongue.

And he had felt this before. But when?

When he first got to the Secret Place alone...

When, only days ago, he had looked at the paintings upon the wall with new eyes.

When he first... Sundeep's face was now screwed up in concentration. When he first ... recognized his mother as one of the Mountainfolk...

When she had climbed high above this place, she had been going home. Had been visiting—

And then he knew. Knew about his mother and father, and how they had died.

And now his tears would not stop.

That evening, he prepared a sack of rations, grasped his father's old stick, and set out once again.

The climb was as quick as Sundeep had anticipated. With

light step, but heavy heart, he reached the Saddle.

Ahead, the old man sat silently on the pinnacle beneath the cave. Sundeep saw how he snatched at passing breaths, his neck craning forward as he did so. He seemed frail and spent, the sturdy timber now turned to fragile ash. Thin grey fingers of smoke reached upwards from the bowl of his pipe, beckoning the moon. Beneath him, a sea of cloud spread in all directions.

Sundeep walked to his side and lowered his pack to the ground, causing a small slough of snow to tumble, mute and fearful, into the void.

And still there was no sign that his approach had been heard, nor his presence observed.

Finally, the old man lowered his pipe and, without turning, spoke.

"You know."

Above, the stars stuttered and stammered in the cold.

Sundeep nodded. "Yes."

He settled slowly on his pack, his back to the pinnacle, looking out and away from the old man, and then down towards his boots.

The old man turned his head. "Tell me."

Sundeep drew breath to speak, sighed, and then tried once more.

"You have told me that you are Ptarmagon. That Awelan, your wife, gave her life so that you might return to your people. That your daughter married a Lowlander and stayed in the valley, where they raised a son."

Ptarmagon nodded.

Sundeep went on.

"Your daughter was Meirwen. My mother."

The old man nodded and lowered his head. Sundeep continued.

"I had to go with her to the Secret Place. And when she climbed onwards from there, it was to visit you and your folk. My mother did not abandon me. My father did not abandon me. They laid down their lives for those they loved. For their family." He paused. "For you."

Ptarmagon nodded once more, stirring at last from his reverie. He clambered stiffly down from the rock, wheezing for breath.

He placed his gnarled hands on Sundeep's shoulders and

seized his gaze. "My boy," he whispered, reaching up to tousle Sundeep's hair as his mother used to do.

And so they stood together, the moonlight drifting across the pinnacle behind them. As the boy's tears subsided, he pressed his head against the old man and felt the rapid rise and fall of his chest, the rattle within.

"So now you know. Meirwen was both your mother and my daughter, and she died for us – for me – in that terrible storm." He shook his head. "A wife and a daughter should not lay down their lives for one such as me. The guilt is hard to bear, as it was for your father. You will remember the sadness in his heart, and also his bitterness.

"But then he, too, laid down his life for us, carrying the widow across the clouds towards the distant mountains." The old man inclined his body out from the ridge towards the suspended moon. "And there he rests."

Sundeep thought again of the night when his father had left; of the lone shooting star that had passed overhead at dawn – the falling coracle that had carried his father and the old widow.

He remembered, too, how he had stood with his mother

one night long ago; his excitement as a shower of shooting stars had drenched the sky with light. And his mother had watched, inconsolable, as her people fell to Earth.

Ptarmagon coughed again and shivered. Sundeep pushed away and examined him closely.

Sweat waxed his brow and beaded his beard, and his skin seemed of tallow.

He smiled weakly.

"Come."

Sundeep passed an arm around Ptarmagon's shoulder and, supporting him, set off towards the cave.

※

The Promise & the Choice

THE CLIMB up the rocky path was slow, Ptarmagon pausing for breath with every few paces and weakening as they went. He stumbled into the cave in a stooped shuffle. The orphan girl looked up from the fire in alarm.

"Morchilla." Ptarmagon coughed violently, his breath sawing and rasping.

Together, Morchilla and Sundeep laid him down on his bedding, the girl cradling his head as he sipped from a wooden bowl.

He smiled. "That's better. So much better. I will be fine."

She smiled in return. "Of course you will."

But their smiles were lies.

When Ptarmagon had drunk, Sundeep took Morchilla's place. Ptarmagon looked up into the boy's eyes. "It is time."

Sundeep shook his head. "But I do not know you yet. It cannot be time."

"It is time," said Ptarmagon again. "I am weary, and can wait only a little longer."

"Then wait," said Sundeep. "Please. Apart from those who live at the coast, I have no one but you."

"And I have only you and Morchilla. Yet, still, it is time."

Sundeep spoke softly. "I will bring you food each day. And fuel for your fire. You need never fear again. I will always be here for you."

"But I cannot always be here for you." Ptarmagon coughed again. "The best has been, and I have been more blessed than ever I deserved. But now I am weary. Were it not for Morchilla and for you, I should have long ago surrendered my soul."

From the corner, Morchilla glanced at them. Ptarmagon looked intensely at Sundeep, and lowered his voice.

"Sundeep. You have one promise to make, and one choice. A promise and a choice."

He spoke firmly.

"You must promise me that you will care for Morchilla. She must never want for anything. Not food. Not shelter." He paused. "And nor must she want for love."

Sundeep nodded.

"Promise me." Ptarmagon grasped his hand, his voice rising to a harsh whisper. "Promise!"

"I promise, Grandfather. You have my word."

Ptarmagon relaxed back onto his mattress. "You are indeed my daughter's son." He coughed, but more weakly now, and slowly closed his eyes.

Sundeep and Morchilla sat with Ptarmagon, tenderly stroking his hair and mopping his brow, whispering to him as he slept. His breathing slowed, his chest rising and falling in weary sighs. Sundeep felt Morchilla's fingers touch and then gently weave amongst his own, and her head sank onto his shoulder.

And so they rested, Ptarmagon, Morchilla and Sundeep.

An hour or so later, Ptarmagon stirred. It took some time for him to focus.

"Still here."

Sundeep smiled.

"You or me?"

Ptarmagon smiled back. "Both."

Against Sundeep's shoulder, Morchilla slept still.

"Grandfather," Sundeep whispered.

There was no answer. Softly, but insistently Sundeep said, "Ptarmagon – the choice?"

Ptarmagon looked confused.

"I had a promise to make, and have done so. But you said there was also a choice."

Ptarmagon nodded. "A choice. As there always is." He paused. "Morchilla is of the Mountainfolk. She can never live in the lowlands. Nor can she forage there, now that the air is no longer pure. If she were to stay here, you would provide for her, perhaps bringing her supplies every few months – she would not need much to survive. But she would be alone, while you dwelled at the coast."

"What would you have me do?"

Ptarmagon shook his head. "Only what is right."

"But you have already told me that she cannot go down the Mountain. And if I were to stay with her here we would both starve, for I would no longer be able to descend to the valley below."

"Then you have one choice to make, but the answer must be your own."

Sundeep was bewildered. "But surely that leaves no choice? No answer?"

Ptarmagon's eyes closed. "There is always an answer. But sometimes the best answer is not the one a man wants to choose."

He was drifting away now, his lips moving softly around one last breath.

"One choice."

Sundeep shook him gently.

But Ptarmagon had gone.

※

The Passing

THE TOOLS, though not his own, were strangely
familiar to the touch. The yeti tooth was sharp in his
grasp, its claw shaping and smoothing in sweeping arcs.

Above, orange burned on ink. Below, Sundeep worked the
frozen river of ice at the crest of the Wall, flakes of fractured
ice lying about him, glinting in the glare of the high moon.

In the cave above, Morchilla slept, silently twitching and
weeping for the man who had cared for her.

Throughout the night, Sundeep worked on, soaked in
starlight, washed by moonlight, drowned in sorrow. There
was no sound but the chip and rasp of ice as he scraped and

sanded. As he worked, the white tide rose from below and the cloud crept in amongst the crags.

At last, his task was done. He climbed to the cave where Morchilla still slept.

He had a choice.

Quietly, he gathered Ptarmagon's possessions and carried them outside. Returning, he lifted the pot of boiled icewater from the fire and carried it to the Pinnacle.

All was prepared.

Inside the cave once more, he rested a hand upon the orphan girl's shoulder. "Morchilla." Her paper-thin eyelids fluttered as she awoke.

He wrapped some skins about her as she stood. "Come."

Together, they carried the body, light as dust, hollow as husk.

Out from the darkness of the cave and into the light of the moon.

Around the narrow ledge.

Round the cornice, their soles scratching the frozen surface like sand.

Along the rocky cliff path, and onto the Saddle.

To the Pinnacle where, twenty feet below, the cloud lapped the mountainshore.

The coracle was already filled with firewood when they laid Ptarmagon's body in it, his arms folded across his chest, his face open to the skies above, his hair brushed by a frosted breeze. And beside him, the yeti claw and tooth. And as the flints sparked the fuel, the ice at first flickered, then danced and roared with light.

Sundeep tipped the pot so that the boiling water struck harsh upon the steep ice beneath the Pinnacle, its splash unleashing a mass of pure white steam that hissed and quenched, forming a steep vapour ramp to the cloud below. And so prepared, Sundeep pushed the coracle from the Saddle above.

At first, it nudged stiffly forwards. But then it began to gather speed, spinning slightly upon its curved base as it slipped down the snow slope. Racing now. Twenty yards, thirty. Blurring, a smear of light.

Lurching over the edge beside the Pinnacle, it was launched onto the thick ramp of steam, accelerating wildly onto the cloud below.

Together, Morchilla and Sundeep stood and watched, his arm around her shoulders and hers around his waist, their heads resting lightly against one another.

The coracle glowed red and gold and green and blue, racing through the mists, trailing a comet-tail of phosphorescence as it plunged beneath the surface.

※

The Final Choice

THE GLOW SETTLED.

Ptarmagon was gone at last, and Morchilla was alone. Alone except for Sundeep.

Sundeep, who had made his promise.

They stood together for some time yet, as the stars eased onwards, shepherded by a full moon.

How long they waited he did not know but, at last, she turned to him, lonely and pitiful. Lost.

"You must leave me." She was weeping. "There are none left here. My people are all gone. I am alone."

He tried to hold her close, but she pushed him away.

"No!" She was crying fiercely now.

"You cannot stay here with me. After only a day, you will not be able to go back to the valleys. And then we would both die for lack of food and fuel."

"I can climb to feed you."

"You cannot! You cannot live the life of a slave. And I have no wish to live the life of a bird trapped in a cage. Go!"

He tried once more to comfort her.

"No! I would rather die than live a prisoner. I must have my death, as you must have your life."

Sundeep pulled her tight against him so that she could not push him away, waiting as her waves of grief pounded his chest.

And slowly, she settled.

He spoke.

"Ptarmagon was right. The answer is not easy. I have but one choice."

He touched her hair, tenderly stroking it smooth against her neck with the palm of his hand.

"I know." She began to sob once more. "You must leave me."

He held her tight.

"I have chosen."

And with that he pushed her gently away from him and turned, his footsteps receding across the snow.

Later that day, Sundeep packed his belongings. It was now nearly a week since he had first climbed the Mountain, and he must set off at once if he was to reach the coast as agreed. His cousins were waiting for him to build a new life with them there.

It was strange. He had never wanted to leave this place, but now he felt settled. Secure. He knew what had become of his parents. Knew that they had loved him. That they had not abandoned him. He would be able to start again in peace.

He gathered those possessions which were most dear to him and put them in his mother's pack: the picture from above the fire, neatly rolled; the yeti tooth and claw; her small silver locket.

Leaving the key to the house above the fire, he took his father's old stick and strode through the door and out past the olive grove.

This time, he did not look back.